CHEETAH FACTS

- Cheetahs have short fur that is a tawny-yellow color with solid black spots.

- Built more like tall, lean racing dogs than other cats, cheetahs have long legs, slender bodies, small heads, and a long tail.

- Cheetahs can run at speeds up to 70 miles per hour, or as fast as a speeding car.

- Unlike other cats, cheetahs cannot fully retract their claws.

- Cheetahs are now found only in certain parts of Africa and Asia.

- In 1900, there were approximately 100,000 cheetahs in Africa and Asia. Due to loss of habitat, there are only 9,000 to 12,000 remaining today.

- Cheetahs normally hunt during the morning and early evening.

- Usually, three to five cubs are born in a litter of cheetahs.

- Cheetah cubs will stay with their mothers for as long as 18 months.

- Generally, cheetahs hunt alone. Occasionally, two or three males may hunt together.

- Cheetahs usually weigh between 80 and 140 pounds, or as much as a large dog.

MUGAMBI'S
JOURNEY

By John Becker
Illustrated by Mark Clapsadle

GINGHAM DOG
P R E S S

Columbus, Ohio

To my grandson Ryan

~ John

To my mother and father, who have always encouraged me, and
to my wife, Joan, and my daughters, Laura and Kristen

~ Mark

Copyright © 2005 School Specialty Children's Publishing. Published by Gingham Dog Press, an imprint of
School Specialty Children's Publishing, a member of the School Specialty Family.

Library of Congress Cataloging-in-Publication Data is on file with the publisher.

Send all inquiries to:
School Specialty Children's Publishing
8720 Orion Place
Columbus, OH 43240-2111

ISBN 0-7696-3167-3

1 2 3 4 5 6 7 8 9 10 PHXBK 09 08 07 06 05 04

A jagged flash of lightning, followed by a loud crackle of thunder, made Mugambi and his sisters snuggle closer together.

Mugambi trembled and burrowed deeper beneath his mother's warm fur where he felt safe.

Cheetahs can be scared sometimes, especially when they are only six weeks old.

Outside their den, the wind moaned and cold rain pelted down. Mugambi, Magara, and Mugesi shivered as they stared into the moonless African night.

In the morning, they would leave their den to travel far away. Their mother had picked up the scent of lions on the breeze. It was not safe to stay.

Lions had discovered their den when Mugambi and his brothers and sisters were very small. Their mother had managed to carry Mugambi, Magara, and Mugesi away, but when she returned for their two brothers, they were gone from the den. The lions had been quicker. That night had been a stormy one, too—like tonight.

When the first warm rays of the Serengeti sun crept into the den, their mother nudged her little ones awake. Her high-pitched chirp, like that of a songbird, meant that it was time to go. Mugambi struggled onto his wobbly legs and hurried to keep up with his mother.

They traveled swiftly across fields of tall, golden-colored grass. Their mother stopped only long enough to sniff the air and twitch her ears. The wisp of a scent or the muffled snapping of a twig might alert her to unseen danger lurking in the grass.

Mugambi also kept watch. Hyenas, wild dogs, leopards, snakes, and eagles could attack a defenseless cheetah cub.

Finally, the cheetah family paused to rest in the shade of a lone acacia tree that stood twisted and gnarled with age. There, Mugambi began to explore on his own. Under the watchful eye of his mother, he climbed to the top of an abandoned termite mound. There, Mugambi got his first view of the vast African landscape. Huge herds of wildebeest and zebra dotted the plain.

A small herd of elephants, their white tusks gleaming in the sunlight, ambled slowly toward a watering hole. Hippos wallowed in gray mud. A group of nimble-footed gazelles parted to let a lone rhino pass. Giraffes curled their tongues between the razor-sharp thorns of a yellow-fever acacia tree to taste its cool, green leaves.

The midday sun became a huge, orange fireball, blazing a hole in the blue sky. Mugambi's black tear stripes under his eyes kept the sun's glare from blinding him.

Their mother made one quick chirp. Mugambi and his sisters knew that this meant they were to stay hidden until she returned. When their mother left them to go hunting, the cubs' only protection was their spotted coats. Yellow fur, speckled with black, allowed the young cheetahs to blend into the surrounding grass.

Their mother had only been gone a short time when a scraggy, unpleasant-looking animal trotted by. It was a young warthog, about the same age as Mugambi and his sisters.

With their sharp tusks, adult wild pigs could be dangerous! This one didn't look dangerous, but when the little warthog spied Mugambi and his sisters, he squealed in alarm.

Instantly, an angry adult warthog broke through the grass, grunting loudly. Mugambi didn't hesitate. He began running with his sisters close behind.

Fortunately, their mother had also been listening. She appeared and quickly guided them through an old, dried-out stream bed.

They continued traveling across the grassy plain until their mother stopped abruptly. For just a moment, she stood as rigid as a statue. Then she pointed her ears forward and immediately flattened her body to the ground among the tall grass—LIONS!

Like their mother, Mugambi and his sisters dropped to the ground, lying as still as spotted stones.

Two hungry female lions were prowling nearby. This was unusual. Lions are normally more active at night.

Mugambi watched his mother tense her muscles. Then, in the blink of an eye, she jumped to her feet and sprinted past the startled lions. Even with her great speed, she was in grave danger at such close range. But this was her only chance to lure the lions away from her babies.

The lions hesitated only for an instant, and then they lunged after her!
Mugambi and his sisters lay quietly without breathing.

Day turned into night, and still their mother did not return. Magara whimpered softly.
As the hours passed, strange sounds filled the night air. Hooting came from a nearby tree,
followed by a frightful screech. Then, a long, mournful howl greeted the full moon. The
moonlight cast an eerie glow over the savanna, making it even more frightening.

Mugambi stood watch while his sisters slept.

Suddenly, something moved nearby. It was coming closer and closer. Mugambi bared his teeth. Breaking through the grass was the shadowy, yet familiar figure of their mother.

The softness of her tongue as she licked Mugambi was proof that his mother was safe—they all were!